Silly Sweet SnuggleBugzzz Dreamzzz

Story by
Pamela Quintana
and **Katherine Johnson**

Illustrated by
Lisa Coddington

Snug As A Bug...In Bed!
www.snugglebugzzz.com

A SnuggleBugzzz Press Book

Published by SnuggleBugzzz Press

Text Copyright © 2010 by SnuggleBugzzz, LLC

Illustration Copyright © 2010 by Lisa Coddington

Photography by Katie Welsh Photography

Cataloguing in Publication Data

ISBN 978-0-615-38169-5

Design: GKS Creative ~ Gwyn Kennedy Snider

Printed in the United States at BookPrintingRevolution.com

To Our SnuggleBugzzz

Justin, Jocelyn and Christopher

All dreams are sweet and
No dreams are silly!

SnuggleBugzzz LOVE when it's

The END of the day!

If you're wondering "WHY?'"

Can you GUESS what they'd say?

Now is that MAGICAL time
Of the NIGHT...
When we WHISPER our WISHES
and hold hands SO tight!

Tucked in SNUG as two Bugzzz
From their TOES to their CHINS
Time for SILLY SWEET dreams...
Now the NONSENSE begins!

Wearing such FANCY pajamas!
Each with a sparkly crown...
Beautiful wings keep them HIGH in the air
Flying over their sweet LITTLE town!

Are they DREAMING of spaceships

Sitting next to their CAT?

ZOOMING high in the SKY!

How CRAZY is that?

Riding bicycles BACKWARDS...

Dreams are so WILLY-NILLY!

Eating ICE CREAM on CLOUDS...

SnuggleBugzzz are so SILLY!

REALLY... what's more SILLY
Than a BATH with a CROCODILE?
BLOWING BUBBLES...SPLISH-SPLASHING
What a RIDICULOUS smile!

How SILLY would THIS be...

A SnuggleBugzzz MARCHING BAND!
In their SWIMSUITS playing trumpets...
As they PARADE across the sand!

They'll DANCE the JITTERBUG
And BOOGIE-WOOGIE to the BEAT!

Which SHOES should they CHOOSE
                For their eight TINY feet?

WOW! WHOA!

Up in the AIR!

What are those Snugglebugzzz DOING up there?

They're HANGING on TIGHT
To the TAIL of a KITE...
Super SILLY fun...
Such a SILLY sight!

Imagine the MAGICAL places they'll GO
    In a BALLOON so EXCITED to see what's BELOW!

MARSHMALLOW mountaintops...
With trees like LOLLIPOPS!

Is that a JELLY BEAN rainbow?
And a CANDY bridge of GUMDROPS?

Before the STARS become SUNSHINE

There's time for one more WISH

It's so hard to pick just ONE...

"Let's HULA-HOOP with a POLKA DOT FISH!"

Of all the SILLY things
They LOVE to do BEST...
It's to SNUGGLE by your side
So you can safely REST!
And if you end EVERY day
With goodnight KISSES and HUGS...

You'll have SILLY SWEET DREAMS
Sleeping next to SNUGGLEBUGZZZ!

SnuggleBugzzz™ are "snuggly" plush toys designed to be your child's
much loved and trusted bedtime companions,
and more importantly
attach to your child's bed sheet creating a block
to help keep your child from rolling off the side of their bed and on to the floor!

Make **SnuggleBugzzz™** part of your child's bedtime routine
and combine the comfort of taking a familiar and cherished friend to bed to hug
and snuggle with the added benefit of placing a block to help keep your child
Snug As A Bug...In Bed!

Buy your SnuggleBugzzz™ at
www.SnuggleBugzzz.com